Samuel French Acting Edition

The Whole Shebang

by Pat Cook

SAMUEL FRENCH

SAMUELFRENCH.COM   SAMUELFRENCH.CO.UK

Copyright © 1995 by Pat Cook
All Rights Reserved

THE WHOLE SHEBANG is fully protected under the copyright laws of the United States of America, the British Commonwealth, including Canada, and all other countries of the Copyright Union. All rights, including professional and amateur stage productions, recitation, lecturing, public reading, motion picture, radio broadcasting, television and the rights of translation into foreign languages are strictly reserved.

ISBN 978-0-874-40478-4

www.SamuelFrench.com
www.SamuelFrench.co.uk

FOR PRODUCTION ENQUIRIES

UNITED STATES AND CANADA
Info@SamuelFrench.com
1-866-598-8449

UNITED KINGDOM AND EUROPE
Plays@SamuelFrench.co.uk
020-7255-4302

Each title is subject to availability from Samuel French, depending upon country of performance. Please be aware that *THE WHOLE SHEBANG* may not be licensed by Samuel French in your territory. Professional and amateur producers should contact the nearest Samuel French office or licensing partner to verify availability.

CAUTION: Professional and amateur producers are hereby warned that *THE WHOLE SHEBANG* is subject to a licensing fee. Publication of this play(s) does not imply availability for performance. Both amateurs and professionals considering a production are strongly advised to apply to Samuel French before starting rehearsals, advertising, or booking a theatre. A licensing fee must be paid whether the title(s) is presented for charity or gain and whether or not admission is charged. Professional/Stock licensing fees are quoted upon application to Samuel French.

No one shall make any changes in this title(s) for the purpose of production. No part of this book may be reproduced, stored in a retrieval system, or transmitted in any form, by any means, now known or yet to be invented, including mechanical, electronic, photocopying, recording, videotaping, or otherwise, without the prior written permission of the publisher. No one shall upload this title(s), or part of this title(s), to any social media websites.

For all enquiries regarding motion picture, television, and other media rights, please contact Samuel French.

Please refer to page 31 for further copyright information.

CHARACTERS

MARGE DORSETT -- A thirty five year old woman who's in charge of a One Act Play festival and a bit on edge.

BETTY HOSKINS -- A teenager who's MARGE'S assistant. She's wise beyond her years.

LILA GRAHAM -- The drama coach from Parkly High. She's in her late forties and something of a she dragon.

KATHREN HOGGADORN -- About the same age and equally as vicious as LILA, she's the drama coach from Slidell High.

MARK HODGES -- The drama coach from Acme High, he is in his mid thirties and overly condescending.

JEREMY COX -- A teenager from Slidell who's portraying "Hamlet."

MILLER BENTLEY -- A teenager from Parkly who's also portraying "Hamlet."

MITCH FRIELAND -- A teenager from Acme, always in his character from "The Tell Tale Heart."

INTERN -- A hospital attendant. (May be played by a man or a woman. Can be doubled with another part.)

TIME: The present.
PLACE: A high school auditorium.

THE WHOLE SHEBANG

(The setting for this slice-of-theater farce is an auditorium. On stage are several practical block units, all painted grey. Included in the units are two small platforms, one taller than the other, a two step stair unit and several chairs.

As the play begins, the main stage is in darkness. A solo LIGHT comes up Downstage Right and illuminates a solitary chair. After a brief pause, an INTERN in a white jacket slowly ushers MARGE to the chair from Stage Left. MARGE is wearing a straight jacket. The INTERN deposits her and, after shaking his/her head, exits Stage Right. MARGE nervously looks around and then her eyes fall on the audience. She smiles benignly.)

MARGE. Psst. Pssssst. Got a minute? How are you? Good, good. Me? Oh, fine, couldn't be better. I saw a bird this morning through the bars. It lit in a tree just outside my cell. I think it was a Blue Jay. Hm? Oh, you're looking at this. *(She tries to raise her arms to indicate the jacket.)* Well, I can explain this. See ... I'm a teacher. *(She shakes her head.)* No, that wasn't what did it. I also drive a school bus. *(She shakes her head again.)* Nope, not that either. I used to teach Drama. *(Shakes her head again.)* That's wasn't it. But you see, last year, we had a one act play contest and they put me in charge. *(She nods vigorously.)* That's the one! *(She suddenly looks around.)* Did you hear that? Like a humming sound. Maybe it was a Hummingbird outside my window.

Sure, that's it. It's doing that just to get me going again. Sure, that's it. (*A solitary tone is heard - the kind of old fashioned tone that used to be used in hospitals. After the tone, a WOMAN'S VOICE is heard in a sterile but grating manner.*)

VOICE. Nothing over forty minutes. Nothing over forty minutes. Thank you. (*The tone sounds again. MARGE pays no attention to this ... at first.*)

MARGE. Oh, I'm okay. It's the others you have to worry about. Oh, sure, you nod but you don't know. You don't understand. Listen to me, I'm just like you. (*She smiles again.*) THAT'S got you thinking, doesn't it? I'm telling you, it's the others you have to worry about. All of them. Standing around, planning, plotting, whining, yelling. Planning, plotting I can take. But whining and yelling? You don't know, you don't understand! And each of them, individually, out to get me! Mocking me! That's it! It was a Mockingbird outside my window! Sure, that's it! (*Another solitary tone is heard.*)

WOMAN'S VOICE. No more than twelve actors in a scene. No more than twelve actors in a scene. Thank you. (*The tone sounds again.*)

MARGE. Yeah, it sounds. And echoes. And builds! Like a drum in your head. That's it! It was a Woodpecker! Outside my window, a Woodpecker! Can't you hear it? That's it, sure, that's it! (*The tone sounds again.*)

WOMAN'S VOICE. All plays must be approved. All plays must be approved. Thank you. (*The tone sounds. MARGE struggles to her feet.*)

MARGE. Stop it! Stop it! (*She remembers the audience.*) Don't you hear that? That ... voice? Constantly! Pounding in my ears, constantly! Sure, that's it! (*She suddenly becomes calm and sits very primly.*) Nice day, isn't it. Breeze out of the north, birds singing. Don't talk to me about birds! It was a day like this when it happened. (*She slowly becomes moody again.*) The council appointed me to run the one act play contest. Piece of cake, they said. A couple of days out of your schedule, they said. Just keep the rule book handy, they said. Somebody with your background and discipline, it's a natural, they said. They just needed somebody responsible for running the whole shebang. That's what they called it, the whole shebang. It's a perfect name for it, too. I was the "she" and it was the "bang." You know, like when a planet explodes! I guess I was already on edge when everyone arrived at once to rehearse onstage. Three schools, three one acts. A piece of cake, they said. Yeah, it was a day just like this one ...

(LIGHTS fade on MARGE and come up on the main stage. The scene is a flurry of activity. BETTY is standing, holding a clipboard. LILA and KATHREN are on both sides of her, talking at once. MARK is standing Stage Left with MITCH and coaching MITCH in deep knee bends and other exercises.)

BETTY. One at time, one at a time!

LILA. We won the drawing of lots, we go first!

KATHREN. (*Same time at LILA.*) Don't go shoving your weight around here!

LILA. So we should have the pick of dressing spaces! When we get through, THEN the others may move in!

KATHREN. EVERYONE gets the same allotted spaces for costumes! But there's no room, now that your hams have taken over the theater!

LILA. Hams! You're one to talk, with the pork you got in your cast. I remember last year ... !

KATHREN. Yeah, when you ripped up my Tartuffe's tights!

LILA. Exactly! Tartuffe's not supposed to HAVE tights! Read the rule book!

KATHREN. I DID read the rule book!

BETTY. Ladies, please! That was last year. This is this year.

KATHREN. Brilliant.

BETTY. And we have to move on …

KATHREN. (*Back to LILA.*) You're only allowed two feet! Two feet of costume space. (*She pulls out and waves a cloth tape measure.*) Not three feet, not two and a half, but TWO!

LILA. You measured? How petty?!

KATHREN. Every inch you stole.

LILA. We CAN'T wrinkle the costumes into a bunch just to please your highness!

KATHREN. It's the rules!

LILA. I tell you, it's impossible unless we shove the clothes carrier into a ball.

KATHREN. Well, shove it, Kathren, shove it!

LILA. Listen, you! (*Betty takes out a referee's whistle and blows it loudly.*)

BETTY. All right! (*The warring ladies stop and look at her.*)

KATHREN. Yes, I resent us being treated like cattle to be whistled at like some pet dogs.

LILA. You're mixing your metaphors.

KATHREN. Yeah, and your breath stinks!

LILA. Look, I can take you the best day you ever had!

KATHREN. Only after you move your costumes!

BETTY. Hey, hey, HEY! (*Again, the coaches get quiet.*) If you have any grievances, please take them up with Miss Dorsett.

LILA. Well, where is Miss Dorsett?

BETTY. I'll go look! (*She crosses Stage Left.*) Marge! Get out here! NOW!

KATHREN. Now you're gonna get it!

LILA. Oh, just shut up! (*MARGE enters warily. She is holding a glass of water and an Alka Seltzer. She looks quickly and drops the tablet in the glass of water. She takes a swallow.*)

KATHREN. I've measured everything we have and taken an inventory too. And I'm going to make sure I put everything we have under lock and key.

LILA. And just what's THAT supposed to mean?

KATHREN. And an armed guard as well, so watch it!

LILA. You are so vindictive!

KATHREN. Shut up! (*They each plop into a chair, with arms crossed defiantly.*)

BETTY. (*To MARGE.*) Where have you been?

MARGE. Looking for a crash helmet. How's it going?

BETTY. (*Sullen.*) You remember the civil war?

MARGE. Sure.

BETTY. You're older than I thought.

MARGE. You're doing a wonderful job, Betty.

BETTY. Same to you! (*She shoves the clipboard into MARGE'S arms and takes the glass. She takes a drink and shoves MARGE.*)

MARGE. Soooo! Nice day out, isn't it? Perfect weather for ... a ... (*She looks down at the coaches.*) ... one ... act ... con ... test. Look, no hand to hand combat, okay? (*LILA and KATHREN begin speaking at once.*)

LILA. Don't tell me, my group was here on time and since we're first I think we should be able to rehearse first.

KATHREN. (*Same time as LILA.*) I resent anyone here

getting preferential treatment. Everyone should be accorded the same space and accommodations!

MARGE. Good. We're talking, that's good. Betty, can I have your whistle? (*BETTY lobs the whistle over to MARGE.*)

BETTY. It won't help.

MARGE. I know but there's a waiting period on pistols now. Now. (*She looks at the clipboard.*) Where are your cast members?

LILA. They're all crammed into those small cubicles you call dressing rooms.

KATHREN. YOU got dressing rooms? My group is out in the hall!

MARGE. Let's just skip over all that, shall we? Now. Who's doing "Hamlet"?

LILA & KATHREN. We are. (*They look at each other.*) We are! (*They both rise.*) You're doing "Hamlet"? We're doing "Hamlet"! (*They both plop back into their chairs.*)

MARGE. You're BOTH doing "Hamlet"? Well, this is going to be fuuuun! (*She crosses to MARK.*) And you're ... ?

MARK. (*Overly condescending.*) Mark Hodges, ma'am. Acme High School. (*Sounds of general disgust from LILA and KATHREN.*)

LILA. Acme high school!

KATHREN. I don't believe it.

LILA. Didn't the roadrunner graduate from there?

MARK. I beg your pardon?

MARGE. And you're NOT doing "Hamlet."

MARK. No ma'am. We've chosen something a bit different?

MARGE. Oh, good. I hope it's something light, a little change of pace, a little humor, something in contrast to... (*She looks at the clipboard.*) You're doing "The Tale Tell Heart"?

MARK. By Edgar Allan Poe, that's right, ma'am.

MITCH. (*In character.*) "The old man was dead! I removed the bed and examined the corpse. Yes, he was stone, STONE dead!"

MARK. And we just wanted to make sure of that we don't step on anyone's toes, theatrically speaking, you understand. And you must be the monitor?

MARGE. That's right. Marge Dorsett.

MARK. Well, if we, in any way, should overstep our limits, I can assure you it is unintentional. Wouldn't want anyone to think I took unfair advantage of anyone, especially someone as charming and, I'm sure, as fair as you, ma'am. (*He smiles amiably.*)

KATHREN. Put it on a cracker, Hodges! You got to stand in line like the rest of us.

LILA. Yeah!

MARGE. Oh, Betty? (*She motions BETTY over. BETTY reluctantly joins her.*)

KATHREN. And don't try any of that soft soap here, either!

BETTY. What?

MARGE. Just for the record, please read the general rules for our illustrious directors.

BETTY. They know the ...

BETTY. Okay, listen up! (*LILA and KATHREN move to BETTY.*)

MARK. Mitch, why don't you go back stage and go over your lines. And remember, we're here as representatives of Acme High.

MITCH. (*Moves Stage Right, quoting.*) "Stealthily, stealthily, until at length a single dim ray, like the thread of a spider, shot out from the crevice and fell upon the vulture eye!" (*He exits.*)

KATHREN. (*Watches MITCH leave.*) Little creep.

MARGE. Mr. Hodges?

MARK. (*Moves to them.*) Yes ma'am, I am all ears. Pray continue.

LILA. You used to sell used cars, right?

MARGE. Betty?

BETTY. (*Rapid-fire.*). Here it is. Nothing over forty minutes. No more than twelve actors in a scene. All plays must be approved. You got it? (*JEREMY enters Stage Right, in costume, and moves to LILA.*)

KATHREN. Oh, I KNOW there's more rules than THAT! (*She waves the tape measure.*) They only get two feet of costume space, five foot square of storage of props and set pieces, including props and scripts and ...

LILA. Oh, here we go again! The Conqueror tape worm in action. (*To KATHREN.*) You keep waving that tape measure in front of me and I'll feed it to you!

MARGE. Ladies, PLEASE!

BETTY. (*Rushes off.*) I better go check the measurements backstage. (*She exits Stage Left.*)

MARGE. (*Fantically.*) Betty!

JEREMY. Mrs. Graham! Mrs. Graham!

LILA. What IS it, Jeremy?

MARGE. This your Hamlet?

LILA. Right.

MARK. And a fine one, he is too.

LILA. Rent a hall, Hodges!

JEREMY. Mrs. Graham, I can't find Yorick.

LILA. What? Yorick's missing?

KATHREN. Foul!

LILA. What do you mean, foul?

KATHREN. You canNOT go outside the script. Yorick was

dead twenty three years beFORE Hamlet begins and here you've written him in to your cutting!

LILA. Just a word of warning, when you leave through the parking lot. I'm driving our van!

MARGE. What's this about adding to the approved script?

LILA. We didn't add ANYthing! We named the skull Yorick and ... (*She realizes.*) The skull's gone?!

JEREMY. That's right. I know we unpacked it but it's disappeared.

LILA. Disappeared, huh? (*She turns savagely and makes a lurch to KATHREN.*) And I can just BET where it's disappeared to!

KATHREN. (*Moves back in reaction.*) Stay away from me! (*MARGE moves quickly and forces herself between the two coaches.*)

MARGE. Just a second! Everybody settle down!

LILA. (*Clawing around MARGE.*) Five minutes! Just five minutes in the prop room and give me a tire tool!

KATHREN. We didn't steal your skull!

MARK. Maybe it was just misplaced. You know how kids are these days. My, my. I could tell you stories ...

LILA. Odd how the one prop, the one MAJOR prop in our piece just happened to vanish!

MARGE. Look, stop it, you two!

LILA. But she has obviously stolen ...

MARGE. Stop it, I said. Look, Mrs. Graham, you can rehearse with something else until we find the skull.

LILA. From where?

KATHREN. She's not getting anything of ours. (*She waves the tape measure again.*) I got everything measured down to the last centimeter.

LILA. (*Clawing again.*) Let me measure you head, we'll

use YOUR skull!

MARGE. Betty?!

KATHREN. T'is a poor workman who blames her tools.

LILA. (*Pleading with MARGE.*) Three minutes, I'll use a can opener!

MARGE. Betty!

BETTY. (*Offstage.*) What?!

MARGE. We need a skull out here! Or something we can use as a substitute for it until we can find one! (*After a slight pause, a volleyball comes bouncing out. MARGE catches it and hands it to JEREMY.*)

MARGE. There you are?

LILA. (*Enraged.*) A volleyball! Jeremy has to rehearse with a volleyball? What's he going to say? "Alas, poor Spaulding, I knew him, Horatio"!

MARGE. We'll find your skull before the contest begins. (*JEREMY moves us and silently rehearses his lines.*)

LILA. You better or I'll lodge a complaint with the council.

KATHREN. Oh, that's your favorite hobby. Lila the Lodger, we call her.

MARK. I don't feel there's any need for ill feelings here, ma'am. We're all part of that great theater experiment and each of us, in our own little way, must do our part and set a good example for the younger members of the troupe.

LILA. Look, Uriah Heep, I've had enough out of you, too! (*MILLER enters Stage Left, also in costume, carrying a skull.*)

MARK. And I fail to see where casting vindictive epithets at each other will profit anybody.

KATHREN. (*Indicates MARK.*) Who TALKS like this?

MILLER. Where can I rehearse, Mrs. Hoggadorn? (*JEREMY sees the skull and moves to MILLER.*)

KATHREN. Oh, Miller. Why don't you go upstage and run

over your part. Then when we get some space, if we ever do ...

JEREMY. Wait a minute. That's our skull.

MILLER. Hah?

MARGE. Wait a minute, you two ...

LILA. What?

MARGE. (*Trying to head it off.*) Just relax a minute here ...

LILA. OUR skull? (*She grabs the skull from MILLER.*) It IS! This is OUR skull!

MARGE. How can you tell one skull from another ... ?

KATHREN. Just what do you think you're doing?!

LILA. It's OUR skull! Here! (*She takes the volleyball and gives it to MILLER.*) Your serve!

KATHREN. You give that back!

MARGE. Ladies...

LILA. Why? You thought a volleyball was good enough for us. YOU try it for awhile!

KATHREN. You ... you THIEF! (*She grabs the skull. LILA hangs on to it and there is a tug of war between the two. MILLER and JEREMY stand next to each other and watch in horror.*)

MARGE. (*Trying to wedge them apart.*) Just a minute ... don't ... you have to let go ...

LILA. Let go!

KATHREN. YOU let go! It's our skull!

LILA. You stole it from us!

KATHREN. Let go of it!

MARGE. Ladies, PLEASE! (*Suddenly, in one large tug, the TWO COACHES pull the skull apart in two large fragments.*)

KATHREN. Oh!

LILA. You ... You broke it!

KATHREN. I broke it?

LILA. I wish to lodge a complaint. Slidell High just fractured my skull!

MARGE. Hey, I can't say I haven't thought of it myself.

MARK. Wait. Maybe we can glue it back together?

KATHREN. Yeah, maybe we can glue your mouth shut!

MARK. Well! (*He moves off and sulks.*)

JEREMY. (*Whining.*) I think I wanna go home.

MILLER. Me, too. (*They takes the volleyball and begin playing catch with it. BETTY enters from the wings, carrying another skull.*)

LILA. First, she tries to measure us out of our space and then she steals our props!

LILA. It was OUR skull!

BETTY. Lookie what I found in the dressing room.

MARGE. What? (*She turns and sees the skull.*) NOW you find it. (*KATHREN and LILA look at the skull and then at each other. Then, at the same time, they both gently put the skull fragments down and then quickly grab the other skull.*)

LILA. You're right, Kathren. THAT'S our skull!

KATHREN. It's ours!

BETTY. I'm outta here! (*She exits quickly.*)

LILA. You said the first one was yours!

KATHREN. Well, you said it was yours!

LILA. This one is ours.

KATHREN. They both look alike. How do you KNOW this one is yours?

LILA. 'Cause yours is broke!

KATHREN. It IS not! THIS is ours!

LILA. It's OURS! (*MARGE, who's had enough, blows the whistle. The ladies stop the tug of war and look at her.*)

MARGE. Okay, that's it! Martial law. (*She grabs the*

skull.) Gimme' that!

LILA. But it's ours!

KATHREN. No, it's ours!

LILA. Ours!

KATHREN. Ours!

MARGE. No, it's MINE! (*She turns, maniacally.*) You hear me! Mine, all mine!

LILA. Wait, you can't ...

MARGE. (*Wheels on her.*) Get away from me! I do hereby confiscate this skull on behalf of the council.

MARK. (*Moves back to them.*) Finally, calmer heads prevail. And it is at a time like this when we all should take a lesson from our monitor here and ...

MARGE. (*Glares at him.*) I got my eye on you too, palie, so watch it!

MARK. (*Retreating.*) Yes ma'am, I only want to do what's right.

MARGE. Now! EACH of you may use this skull when it's time for your one act. So let it be written, so let it be done. (*She turns to the two Hamlets.*) And stop that dribbling back there! (*JEREMY catches the ball and he and MILLER become. very meek. They then begin going over their lines quietly.*)

LILA. So we're now to follow rules that AREN'T in the rule book, is that it?

MARGE. (*Guttural.*) You want to use a volleyball?

LILA. No, but ...

MARGE. Then, shut up! What IS it with you two? We're supposed to be adults here! Aren't we? (*LILA and KATHREN look at each other.*) Well? Don't you think it's time we ACTED like adults?

LILA. (*After a slight pause.*) I was but she wasn't.

KATHREN. Was so!

LILA. Was not!

KATHREN. (*Rushes at MARGE.*) Gimme' that skull!

MARGE. (*Moves back.*). Get away from me!

KATHREN. But it's ours!

LILA. No, it's ours! Give it to me!

MARGE. Back! Back, I said. (*She raises the skull high over her head.*) One more move and this'll be toothpicks!

LILA. But we ... !

MARGE. Back! Go on! Get! (*LILA and KATHREN retreat reluctantly. MARGE lowers the skull.*)

KATHREN. I can't believe we're being treated like ...

MARGE. Go on! Sit down! SIT! (*LILA and KATHREN sit.*)

MARK. Maybe I ought to hold the skull. (*He reaches for it.*)

MARGE. (*Growling.*) Get away from me!

MARK. (*Hurt.*) Just trying to help. (*He moves away.*) (*MARGE now holds the skull like a pitcher checking the bases. She looks at KATHREN and then at LILA and then, quickly, back at KATHREN. She relaxes a bit and looks at the skull.*)

MARGE. (*To the skull.*) How do you put up with this? Does this go on all the time? (*BETTY enters, now wearing a knight's armor chest plate and helmet. She moves to MARGE and watches her. MARGE continues her conversation with the skull.*) All this grief and over what? A prop. Just a piece of plastic. Why're you smiling at me like that? You think it's funny?

MARGE. What?!

BETTY. Why're you talking to that skull?

MARGE. Hah? (*She looks at the skull.*) Oh, this? Nothing. I was just talking to myself and ... what're you wearing?

BETTY. I found a bunch of armor backstage. I think it was left over from when we did "Richard the Third". (*Proudly.*) I played the Earl of Surrey.

MARGE. Who cares?

BETTY. I thought it might be a good idea to put it on. Listen, there's a lot more back there if you need it. And it's all the real stuff, too. Swords, battle axes, the whole shebang.

MARGE. Don't say those words to me. (*She shoves the skull into BETTY'S arms.*) Now. Let's get organized. We're only got about thirty minutes before this thing begins. (*She pulls a chair over and sits.*) Hodges?

MARK. Yes ma'am?

MARGE. Sit down. (*BETTY crosses and picks up the skull fragments off the stage.*)

MARK. Yes ma'am. (*He sits in a chair.*)

MARGE. (*To herself.*) Nothing over forty minutes, they said. No more than twelve actors in a scene, they said. Keep it relaxed, they said. My head feels like it's coming apart.

BETTY. Like this? (*She holds up a fragment.*)

MARGE. Never mind. By the way, what happened to the lady who ran this thing last year?

BETTY. (*Matter-of-factly.*). She died.

MARGE. I don't want to know how either, do I?

LILA. Miss Dorsett?

MARGE. What?

LILA. If there's only thirty minutes left before the contest starts, then we don't have time to rehearse now, do we?

MARGE. No, I guess you don't.

KATHREN. You mean you deliberately wasted time so that we have to perform cold?

MARGE. (*Jumps up.*) Me?!

LILA. Mrs. Handley had everything organized last year and

it ran like clockwork.

MARGE. Mrs. Handley?

BETTY. She's the one that ... (*She sticks out a thumb and turns it down.*)

MARGE. Self inflicted wound, I'll bet.

KATHREN. (*Jumps up.*) Look, Miller has to run over the scene with the skull.

LILA. (*Also jumps up.*) Well, so does Jeremy.

KATHREN. But Miller just came in at the last minute and took over the role.

LILA. You heard her! No special treatment. Let's see you tape measure your way out of this.

KATHREN. Miss Dorsett!

MARGE. Fine. Get them over there. Both of them! (*She moves to the platforms.*)

LILA. What?

KATHREN. Both of them? At the same time?

MARGE. Over here! Let's go!

MARK. Now that's a capitol idea.

MARGE. Come on! (*She motions to JEREMY and MILLER. They move to her.*)

LILA. (*To MARK.*) Doesn't your lead need rehearsing?

MARK. (*Casually.*) He knows his lines.

LILA. That's it! (*She rushes to MARK and grabs his neck.*) I've had it with Mr. Smug here! (*She throws MARK out of the chair and onto the stage floor.*)

MARGE. MRS. GRAHAM! Stop it! (*She rushes over and pulls LILA off MARK.*)

KATHREN. (*Moves to the fray.*) Kick him while he's down! One for me!

MARK. Somebody HELP me!

MARGE. Mrs. Graham, get OFF him!

BETTY. I'm getting the battle ax! (*She rushes off Stage Left.*)

MARGE. Get up! Come on, get up! (*She shoves LILA to one side.*)

LILA. (*Panting.*) I hate condescension!

MARK. What does rain have to do with anything?

LILA. What?

KATHREN. The man's an idiot. He's smug and he's an idiot.

MARGE. Okay, you two! You! (*She moves LILA to Stage Right of the platforms near JEREMY.*) Stand over here and don't move! (*She moves back to KATHREN.*) And you! (*KATHREN quickly moves to Stage Left of the platforms near MILLER.*)

KATHREN. I go over here, right?

MARGE. That's right and don't move unless I call you, you miserable ...

KATHREN. Of course. (*KATHREN smiles weakly and, during the next few speeches, begins measuring the platforms.*)

MARGE. (*Helps MARK up.*). Are you all right?

MARK. I ... I think so. They really take all this seriously, don't they.

MARGE. As a heart attack. (*She feels her chest.*) And why did I say that?

MARK. Well, I can assure you that you'll get no grief from me.

MARGE. Will you put that in writing?

LILA. (*Pointing to KATHREN.*) She's doing it again! She's measuring the platforms! She's measuring the platforms! (*She rushes around the platforms and begins chasing KATHREN.*)

KATHREN. Just checking! There's nothing in the rule

books against us checking the ... (*She runs away from LILA.*) What do you think you're doing?! Stay away from me!

LILA. I'm going to take that stupid tape measure and ram it right down your lying, thieving throat! (*They are now circling the platforms. MILLER and JEREMY keep their eyes on them, their bodies turning to follow the action.*)

MARGE. Stop it! You hear me?

JEREMY. (*A race track announcer.*) And they're coming around the clubhouse turn ...

MILLER. Run, Mrs. Hoggadorn, run!

JEREMY. And it looks like Hoggadorn is losing steam in the home stretch ...

LILA. You can't run forever!

KATHREN. I can outrun you, you old windbag!

LILA. Yeah? You gotta' sleep sometime! (*MARGE rushes over to the platforms. She waits for KATHREN to pass and then sticks out her leg.*)

KATHREN. You're just jealous of our record!

LILA. What record?! The only way YOU can win is if you measure all the opposition out of the running! You can't win when it's just your cast and ... Oop! (*MARGE trips LILA and she crashes to the floor. KATHREN stops and leans on the platform, out of breath. MARK rushes over to the group.*)

MARGE. Did you hurt yourself?

LILA. Yes! (*She rubs her elbows.*)

MARGE. Goooood! (*BETTY enters quickly, carrying a short handled battle ax. She hands it to MARGE and exits the same way.*)

KATHREN. She's crazy! That old bat's crazy!

LILA. Old bat?! Why, you ... ! (*She starts to get up. MARGE quickly holds the ax near her.*)

MARGE. I would make any sudden moves if I were you.

(*LILA looks at the ax and lays back down.*)

MARK. I have never seen such behavior. And I've studied Orangutans.

KATHREN. What's that mean?

MARK. Well, all this fuss over who gets what?   And which cast gets to be first?

MARGE. It IS ridiculous!

MARK. Right. After all, Mrs. Graham got first lot so she gets to be first.

KATHREN. You dirty, low life! I'll kill you!   (*She grabs MARK and forces him on his back onto a platform.*)

MARK. Somebody HELP me!

MARGE. Mrs. Hoggadorn!   (*She rushes over and, after leaning the ax against the platform, begins to pull KATHREN off MARK.*) Stop it!

MILLER. Should we help?

JEREMY. (*Shakes his head.*) Take it from me. I've been here before.

KATHREN. Lying newcomer! Comes in here and takes sides! What do YOU know, anyway?! (*MARGE wrenches her away from MARK.*)

MARGE. Mrs. Hoggadorn! Now, stop it right this minute!

MARK. I can't believe this! (*He lurches away from KATHREN and moves toward LILA. He turns just in time to see LILA jump to her feet and move toward him. He quickly moves away from her.*)

MARGE. Mrs. Graham! (*She grabs the ax.*) Don't make me use this!

LILA. (*Stops.*) You don't have the guts.

MARGE. (*Vehemently.*)   No jury in the world would convict me.

KATHREN. Lila! Careful. (*She eyes MARGE.*) I think she

means it.

MARGE. (*The Wicked Witch of the West.*) Just TRY to keep away from me, just TRY. I'll get you, my pretty! (*LILA tries a new tack, becoming calm and a bit. Patronizing.*)

LILA. Okay, Miss Dorsett. Sure. Whatever you say. We'll behave ourselves, won't we, Kathren?

KATHREN. Uh ... sure. After all, she's in charge here, right?

LILA. That's right. (*She inches her way to her feet.*) And we're all going to do everything we can to help her, right? (*KATHREN, catching on, slowly moves up behind MARGE.*)

KATHREN. That's right, that's right.

LILA. After all, we're all here after the same thing. We all want the contest to run smoothly, don't we? (*LILA'S smooth words have an almost hypnotizing influence on MARGE. She watches LILA cautiously but slightly dazed. She begins to waver from side to side as if watching a cobra.*)

KATHREN. (*Moving closer to MARGE.*) Sure, that's it. And we're all professionals, right?

LILA. That's right, sure. We're all here to help you. (*She moves closer to MARGE.*)

MARGE. You are?

LILA. Sure.

KATHREN. (*Almost behind MARGE.*) That's right. We right behind you ... all the way.

LILA. Sure. Nothing to worry about now, is there? (*KATHREN raises her arms to grab MARGE from the back when MARK calls out.*)

MARK. Miss Dorsett! Look out! Behind you! (*MARGE wheels around just as KATHREN lunges for her. MARGE successfully side steps her and she collides with LILA.*)

LILA. OOHP!

MARGE. Ah HA! Thought you had me that time, didn't you?

LILA. (*Shoves KATHREN over.*) Get OFF me!

KATHREN. We almost had her.

MARGE. So THAT'S the way it's going to be. (*She backs away from the two. MARK moves to her.*)

MARK. That was a close one.

KATHREN. (*Threateningly.*) We'll remember you, Hodges. Don't ever forget that.

MARGE. Okay, now listen to me, ALL of you! We're going to rehearse this one scene and that's it. This thing starts on time ... (*She looks at MARK*) ... no ifs, ands ... (*She looks at KATHREN and LILA.*) ... or buts!

KATHREN. Why did you look at us when you said that last part?

MARGE. All right. You! (*To LILA.*) Back where you were. (*To KATHREN.*) You, too! (*LILA and KATHREN resume their positions on opposite sides of the platforms.*)

LILA. Rehearsing the same scene at the same time, that's the most ridiculous thing I ever heard.

KATHREN. This is a farce, if you ask me. I've never been treated so horribly.

MARGE. (*To MARK.*) You got anything else you need? Does what's his name need to run through anything?

MARK. We came prepared. That's what it's all about, isn't it?

LILA. I-I-I-I HATE you!

MARGE. Hamlets?

JEREMY & MILLER. Yes ma'am?

MARGE. Begin! (*The two Hamlets look at their respective coaches. LILA and KATHREN nod and they begin. JEREMY & MILLER begin the same speech, each paying attention to their coach's shouts while they continue.*)

JEREMY & MILLER. (*In unison.*) "Alas, poor Yorick. I knew him, Horatio. A fellow of infinite jest, of most excellent fancy. He hath borne me on his back a thousand times and now, how abhorred in my imagination it is! My gorge rises at it. Here hung those lips that I have kissed, I know not how oft. Where are your gibes now? Your gambols? Your songs? Your flashes of merriment, that were wont to set the table on a roar? Not one now, to mock your own grinning? Quite chap fallen? Now get you to my lady's chamber and tell her, let her paint an inch thick, to this favor she must come, make her laugh at that!" (*Just after the Hamlets begin their speech, LILA and KATHREN start shouting stage directions at their two stars.*)

LILA. Louder, Jeremy! Louder and with feeling! Face the audience! Don't drop your gaze, keep eye contact! More feeling there! Keep it lively but still with that feeling! Don't underplay that, it's important! Let us hear your anguish! Nice, nice but don't pout! You're dropping your gaze again! Keep it moving, keep it moving! Don't lose the center of the character! Too subtle, too subtle! Louder! and with feeling!

KATHREN. (*Same time as LILA.*) More volume, Miller! Make those tones heard throughout the theater! Don't bite off the ends of your words like that! Keep it moving! Don't slouch, stand up to the words! Speak to both the dead and the living! The audience, don't forget the audience! Breeeathe! You hear? Breeeathe! In and out, in and out! That's it! Don't swallow! You're wandering, don't wander! Stand your ground! Where's your accent? Round tones, remember, round tones! (*MARK talks with MARGE, beginning just after LILA and KATHREN start their speeches.*)

MARK. (*Loudly.*) Isn't Hamlet a bit overdone?

MARGE. What?

MARK. Isn't the play Hamlet a bit overdone? I mean, aren't the judges tired of it?

MARGE. What do THEY know? One's an orthodontist and the other's a garage mechanic.

MARK. THOSE are the JUDGES?

MARGE. Everybody else has real jobs! (*BETTY enters with MITCH. MITCH is now in costume.*)

BETTY. Marge! (*They move to MARGE.*)

MARGE. What?

BETTY. Junior here lost his heart!

MARGE. What?!

MARK. The heart's missing?

MARGE. What did you say? He lost his WHAT?

MITCH. The heart! At the end of "The Tell Tale Heart" I pull out this Plaster of Paris heart! But it's gone!

MARK. It was right there in the van in a box!

MITCH. I know but it's not there!

BETTY. First, a skull and now a heart?! We should be doing this for morticians!

MARK. Somebody stole it! I know it was there when we drove up this morning!

MARGE. Not again! (*She is weakening amid all the noise.*) This is getting to me. I'm telling you, this is getting to me! (*The NOISE grows louder and more frantic.*)

BETTY. (*To MARK.*) Don't you have a back up heart?

MARK. Who brings a back up heart to a One Act Play Festival?

BETTY. Can you use something else?

MARGE. We have something else he can use?

BETTY. We got a rubber pig.

MARK. "The Tell Tale Pig"?

BETTY. We got a lot of fast drying paint. We could paint it!

MARK. You don't think the judges can tell the difference between a heart and a red pig?!

BETTY. I didn't say we had red!

MARGE. Piece of cake, they said! Couple of days, they said!

MARK. (*To MITCH.*) You sure you didn't move it somewhere?!

MITCH. No sir. I only did what you said.

MARK. What?

MITCH. I SAID I ONLY DID WHAT YOU SAID.

MARK. WHAT DID YOU DO?

MITCH. I MOVED THAT SKULL INTO THE DRESSING ROOM!

MARK. WHAT? (*Suddenly the speeches finish, the other coaches stop shouting but MITCH continues to shout.*)

MITCH. I MOVED THAT SKULL INTO THE DRESSING ROOM LIKE YOU SAID!

MARGE. (*Quietly.*) You? You moved the skull? (*She turns to MARK.*)

MARK. I ... I only ... well, see I thought.

LILA. (*Renewed vehemence.*) HE'S the one?

KATHREN. HE stole our skull? (*LILA and KATHREN move, slowly at first, then picking up speed, toward MARK.*)

MARK. Well, it was just lying there and I thought ... well, I figured somebody might trip over it, so I ...

LILA. GET HIM! (*LILA and KATHREN rush MARK. He runs around the platforms, followed closely by the other two coaches.*)

KATHREN. I'll kill him!

MARK. Wait! No, don't!

LILA. Running won't do you any good!

KATHREN. I'll kill him!

MARK. Stay away from me! Miss Dorrrrrsssettt!

LILA. He's mine. Two minutes and give me a chain saw!

KATHREN. Not before me! (*BETTY notices MARGE is now staring wide-eyed off in a distance and fingering the ax.*)

BETTY. Marge? Marge, aren't you going to DO anything? Marge?

MARGE. Yeah. Yeah, it's time. (*She slowly moves to the platforms.*)

LILA. We're gaining on you, Hodges! We're gaining on you!

KATHREN. Stop and take it like a man!

MARK. Help me! SOMEBODY HELP ME!

LILA. Don't fight it, Hodges! You wanted to play in the big leagues!

KATHREN. Don't crowd me, Lila! (*MARGE stands with her back to the audience. When. MARK runs by her, she trips him. With predicted results, LILA and KATHREN also trip and fall on MARK. MARGE moves to them and, again with her back to the audience, and looks down at them.*)

LILA. What's she doing??!!

KATHREN. Mrs. DORSETT??!! (*MARGE raises the ax high over her head.*)

BETTY. MAAARRRGE! NOOO! (*Just before MARGE can bring the ax down the LIGHTS BLACK OUT. After a pause of one beat, BETTY'S voice is heard in the darkness.*)

BETTY. (*Calmly.*) Good evening, ladies and gentlemen, and welcome to the Fiona Handley Memorial One Act Play festival. One brief announcement. Because of a few technical … and medical problems, there will be a slight change in our line up. The first play this evening will be "The Tell Tale

Heart." Thank you. (*A solo LIGHT comes up Downstage Left. MITCH walks into the LIGHT and begins his speech.*)

MITCH. (*Maniacally.*) "True, ... nervous ... very, very dreadfully nervous I have been and am, but why will you say that I am mad? No, it is this way. The ... the disease! Yes, the disease had sharpened my senses, not destroyed, not dulled them. (*The LIGHT dims on MITCH and a solo LIGHT comes up Downstage Right, where MARGE sits, again in her straight jacket.*) Above all was the sense of hearing acute. I heard all things in heaven and in earth. How, then, can you say that I am mad ... ? (*The LIGHT on MITCH BLACKS OUT.*)

MARGE. You can see how it was. Sure, that's it. Sure. But ... you knew this already, didn't you? You ALL knew! Piece of cake they said. A couple of days, they said. (*The INTERN enters, smiling, and helps her to her feet. She speaks to him.*) A responsible person, they said. Sure, that's it. And the voices! You can hear them, can't you? You can hear them, too, can't you? Sure, that's it. The voices. (*The tone sounds.*)

VOICE. Nothing over forty minutes. Nothing over forty minutes. Thank you. (*The tone sounds.*) No more than twelve actors in a scene, no more than twelve actors in a scene. Thank you. (*The tones sounds. As the INTERN and MARGE exit, the LIGHT dims.*) All plays must be approved. All plays must be approved. Thank you. (*Tone.*) Thank you. (*Tone.*) Thank you ... (*The LIGHTS dims out and ends the play.*)

THE END

MUSIC USE NOTE

Licensees are solely responsible for obtaining formal written permission from copyright owners to use copyrighted music in the performance of this play and are strongly cautioned to do so. If no such permission is obtained by the licensee, then the licensee must use only original music that the licensee owns and controls. Licensees are solely responsible and liable for all music clearances and shall indemnify the copyright owners of the play(s) and their licensing agent, Samuel French, against any costs, expenses, losses and liabilities arising from the use of music by licensees. Please contact the appropriate music licensing authority in your territory for the rights to any incidental music.

IMPORTANT BILLING AND CREDIT REQUIREMENTS

If you have obtained performance rights to this title, please refer to your licensing agreement for important billing and credit requirements.

www.ingramcontent.com/pod-product-compliance
Lightning Source LLC
Chambersburg PA
CBHW070404120726
47909CB00008B/2988